TRIA VIA JOURNAL 1
Light Sliding Through Space

SHARE
RESOURCES INC

Published by:
SHARE**snacks** an imprint of SHARE Publishing
The TRIA VIA Journals™ is a trademark of Share Resources Inc.
For information address Share Resources Inc., Calgary, Alberta, Canada.
www.shareresourcesinc.com

ISBN 978-1-989269-00-8 (paperback)
ISBN 978-1-989269-04-6 (ebook)

First Edition

The TRiA ViA journals™ are stories of the adventures
of three trip-happy girls named Mia, Lia & Sophia.
The girls often begin swirling and enter another
world called the Kingdom of Whirl. They have delightful
adventures in the Kingdom of Whirl with light, sound, colour
and whimsical substances because everything there is alive.

Follow along as they discover a whole new realm,
exploring new places and meeting new people
from the comfort of their everyday life.

Visit Mia, Lia & Sophia at:
www.thetriaviajournals.com

Written by Angela Thunket
www.angelathunket.com

This journal is *dedicated* to Peritiel, the messenger who brought
this story out of the Kingdom of Whirl for this book on the ground.
Thank you for your experience.

— ANGELA THUNKET

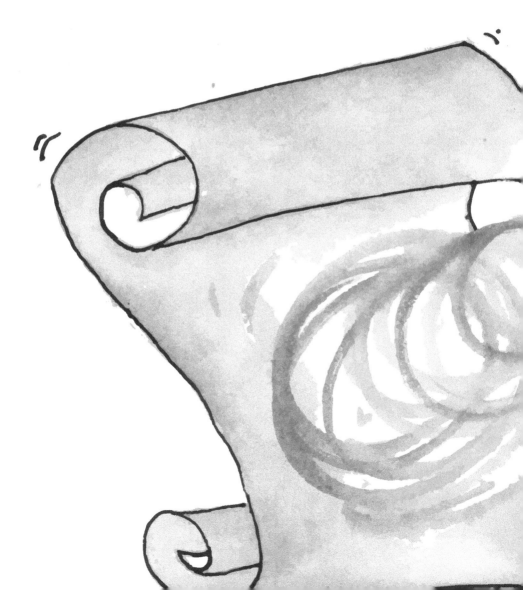

Once along a timeline, in a kingdom so near,
three young girls began swirling without any fear.

Now Mia and Lia and Sophia spent days,
having many fun trips with the King of all ways.

For they knew how to swirl by themselves forever,
although swirling was far more fun when together.

As they shared of a fun swirly trip they each had,
they all started again to unravel a tad.

They wondered if others would also like to swirl,
When reading of some trips to the Kingdom of Whirl.

And so now it was time that they wrote some journals,
For the sharing of swirls of three trip happy girls.

Once Sophia had been swirling through some tube slides,
That were far better than some amusement park rides.

At the end of the slide, she had felt very wise,
She told Mia and Lia with big open eyes,

And to her it was much
like a long waterslide,
Like a rollercoaster
that was not very wide.

Lia heard this and shared
of a slide like that too,
But for Mia the idea
was all brand new.

She too wanted to ride on a slide in a swirl,
So, she went to look into the Kingdom of Whirl.

The great King of Whirl loved to share his grand kingdom,
And she went to ask him if they could go find some.

His smile beamed as she made her first sliding request,
And together they swirled to find some of the best.

Soon they found a big door to a tunnel of light,
And Mia blurted out a small squeal of delight.

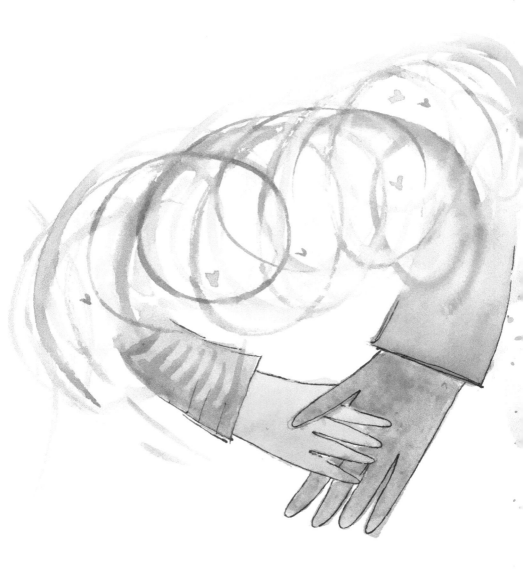

Mia held the King's hand as they went together,
They were sliding much faster than Mia had ever.

Inside was very bright and a little too fast,
And Mia could not see if the King had gone past.

When at last she stopped sliding
she knew they had gone,
So far out in the night
that they went past the dawn.

She called out for the King,
who appeared from inside her,
They had swished and then mashed,
and were sort of a blur.

He said where she landed would not be a worry,
in his kingdom, the time did not have to hurry.

They stood looking out over a huge black ocean,
When tiny lights began to twinkle in motion.

As the lights grew much
brighter they began to sway,
Until the whole ocean was
as bright as twelve days.

Then the King shared how
she could return anytime
By simply remembering their
swirl in her mind.

He showed the end of the slide
where the ocean once sneezed,
And she could come back here
with her friends if she pleased.

They might start to meet others
in this special place,
While exploring the kingdom,
light-sliding through space.

Mia knew the light-slide
was happy to be found,
For when she said thank you,
it was twirling around.

It was spinning and turning,
inside and then out,
Flipping over and over
and twirling about.

Colours shot from the slide when it turned all aroun[d]
As if they were dancing to their very own sound.

Mia danced with the slide and she joined in the twi[rl]
Then she turned inside out which is odd for a girl.

Soon she saw colours
were shooting out of her too,
From the inside and out,
she turned gold, white and blue.

This was so much fun
she was excited to share
With her friends on the ground,
how the colours danced there.

After hours of *dancing*
in the bright black ocean,
She was ready for home
now full of emotion.

Then she blurred with the King
as they entered the slide,
Expecting to *go fast*
on this light speeding ride.

She never knew that colour
was alive in the night
And when they mixed together
they would smile as one light.

She was full of delight
only wanting to sing
When they landed back near
the great throne of the King

In her mind, she could hear a large choir full of sound
And a song that had never been heard on the ground.

So, she started to sing all the sounds from her belly,
When she opened her mouth, they flowed out like jelly.

For a while she wobbled
in the Kingdom of Whirl,
Knowing soon she would surely
be finished her swirl.

And the King was so happy
that they were a blur,
For now, Mia knew clearly
she was not just her.

She wondered if Lia and Sophia blurred too,
Or if everyone could be a Blur if they knew?

As she swirled to the ground in her comfy chair frame,
Then she wondered if sound jelly might have a name?

She would have to go back 'till she learned more and more,
About how to bring sound jelly through the King's door.

Mia sat in her chair full of joy and delight,
But found no time had passed since her light-sliding flight.

Like always happened when she went up for a swirl,
She had more questions now of the Kingdom of Whirl.

The girls shared all they knew
every time they saw more,
Then they tripled the fun
as they swirled and explored.

They all thought of a fancy new name for themselves,
For the swirls of three girls and their journals on shelves.

From then on, the two others along with Mia,
Went swirling together as TRiA ViA.

WATCH FOR THESE NEW TRIA VIA Journals™

www.thetriaviajournals.com

TRIA VIA JOURNAL 2
Gardens Galore
We found a garden with
a heart for a door!

TRIA VIA JOURNAL 3
Dragons at the Gates
A dragon ate our treasures
so we went to get them back!

TRIA VIA JOURNAL 4
We Met Ourselves Again
Now, is when the future meets the past!

TRIA VIA JOURNAL 5
Crown Cities on Air
Finding new ways to shine!

TRIA VIA JOURNAL 6
Thinking Out Loud
Our thoughts made
things come alive!

TRIA VIA JOURNAL 7
Scrolling for Scrolls
What do we do with
all of these scrolls!

AND STILL MORE NEW **TRIA VIA** Journals,
www.thetriaviajournals.com

WATCH FOR THESE NEW  TRIA VIA Journals™

TRANSLATIONS

German

Sprechen sie Deutsch?

Achten Sie auf diese neuen Übersetzungen

Portuguese

você fala português?

cuidado com essas novas traduções

TRIA = three, elect, sift, sample, put on trial, to prove

VIA = pathway or route

Journals = diary, logbook, chronicle

ANGELA THUNKET

Angela has been fascinated by rhyme since the beginning of time. She lives in Canada and loves to swirl and twirl and whirl. She also likes chocolate peanut butter ice cream, fun beats, melodies, telling stories, friends and laughing. She really likes laughing a lot.

www.angelathunket.com

LEE-ANN LUKACS

Lee-Ann and her family live in Canada and enjoy creating all the time. She loves light and sound and colour. She also likes music, singing, blueberries, painting, nature and having fun. She really likes having fun a lot.

www.thelightcreative.ca

CPSIA information can be obtained
at www.ICGtesting.com
Printed in the USA
LVHW070342141220
674086LV00011B/192